MW01056202

Christmas Is... For Me!

CHRISTINE TANGVALD

ILLUSTRATED BY **TONY GRIEGO**

BETHANY BACKYARD®
www.bethanyhouse.com

Christmas Is... **For Me!**

Text © 2000 by Christine Tangvald

Illustrations © 2000 by Bethany House Publishers

Design and production by Lookout Design Group, Inc. (www.lookoutdesign.com)

Published by Bethany House Publishers

11400 Hampshire Avenue South

Bloomington, Minnesota 55438

www.bethanyhouse.com

Bethany House Publishers is a division of

Baker Publishing Group, Grand Rapids, Michigan.

Printed in China.

ISBN 0-7642-2337-2

Library of Congress Cataloging-in-Publication Number applied for

Did you know that Christmas is ? It is.

I really like Christmas, don't you?

I like to see the twinkling lights on our Christmas tree.

I like to hear the sounds of bells at Christmastime.

And I really like Christmas  presents, don't you?

We use all these things at Christmastime.

We call them *symbols*. And each symbol has

its very own story . . . just For Me!

Do you have a Christmas at your house?
tree

I love our Christmas . It's !
tree   green

 is the color for EVERLASTING—did you know that?
Green

It's like God's
love

God's is EVERLASTING. That means God will me
love   love

FOREVER and EVER and EVER!

(And FOREVER is a long, long time.)

I'm glad my Christmas is , aren't you?
tree   green

God's everlasting love is **For Me!**

JEREMIAH 31:3; PSALM 23:6

One decoration I put on my Christmas is a .

tree   bell

 make sounds.

Bells   happy

Ring, dong, ding, dong.

 tell me about JOY.

Bells

The sound of is the sound of joy . . .  .

bells

Oh, yes. I like to put on my Christmas .

bells   tree

Ring, dong, ding, dong.

Bells make sounds of joy **For Me!**

ROMANS 15:13; PSALM 95:1

Grandma uses pretty 🕯️🕯️ (candles) at her house at Christmas.

I like 🕯️🕯️ (candles), don't you?

We light our 🕯️🕯️ (candles) with a 🔥 (match).

A little flame burns like this: 🔥.

The 🕯️ (candle) gives off pretty 🔥 (light).

The 🔥 (light) of the 🕯️ (candle) tells me that 👤 (Jesus) is the 🔥 (Light) OF THE 🌍 (world)!

👤 (Jesus) is a 🔥 (light) for you and a 🔥 (light) **For Me!**

YAY! HOORAY!

Jesus is the Light of the World!

JOHN 8:12

We have a round  on our front door.

wreath

Sometimes we bake Christmas cookies shaped like .

wreaths

A  is round — like a circle.

wreath

It goes around and around . . . forever.

Can you trace it with your finger?

It has no beginning and NO END.

That's how God's ♥ is **FOr Me!**

love

It has NO BEGINNING and NO END.

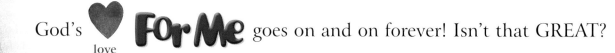

God's ♥ **FOr Me** goes on and on forever! Isn't that GREAT?

love

God's love for me goes on and on forever!

JOHN 3:16; PSALM 139:1–18

Did you know that Christmas is birthday? It is.
Jesus'

HAPPY BIRTHDAY, !
Jesus

Long ago, was born in a
baby Jesus   stable

in the town of .
Bethlehem

 and were there, too.
Mary   Joseph

It was GOD'S PLAN!

(I wish I could have been there, too . . . don't you?)

Christmas is Jesus' birthday!

LUKE 2:1–19

The night was born, God sent lots of to tell
baby Jesus   angels

the  about , His Son.
shepherds   Jesus

"Glory to God in the highest!" sang the .
angels

Do you think the were surprised?
shepherds

Do you think the were happy?
shepherds

Yes! They were!

Angels sang songs to the shepherds!

LUKE 2:8-14

On that same night, God made a bright 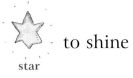 to shine
star

down where was born.
baby Jesus

God's beautiful Christmas twinkled and shined.
star

Oh, MY! It was the BRIGHTEST in the sky.
star

Three followed the to find .
wise men   star   baby Jesus

The 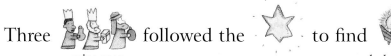 brought beautiful 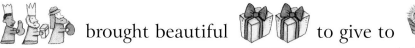 to give to .
wise men   presents   baby Jesus

God's bright star led the wise men to baby Jesus.

MATTHEW 2:1–11

Do you like to get  for Christmas? I do!

And I like to give  for Christmas, too.

But God gave us the BEST CHRISTMAS  of all!

Did you know that?

God gave us His Son, , to be our and SAVIOR!

Oh, yes! is my VERY OWN Christmas .

He is MY AND SAVIOR!

Thank you, God, for !

Jesus is my special Christmas present from God.

JOHN 3:16; ROMANS 6:23

We use all the Christmas symbols to celebrate

the birth of .

baby Jesus

The Christmas 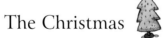 means God gives me

tree

EVERLASTING  .

love

The sound of tells me of the JOY of Christmas.

bells

Pretty  tell me that Jesus is the Light OF THE world.

candles   Jesus   Light   world

The wreath tells me that God's love goes on FOREVER.

wreath   love

Christmas presents tell me that God gave His Son, Jesus,

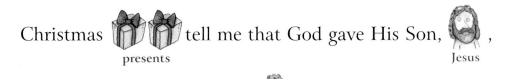

presents   Jesus

to be my very own Friend and SAVIOR!

Friend

But the best part is that Christmas is . . .

 was born . . . FOR ME!

Jesus

Thank you, God.

Thank you,  .

baby Jesus

Merry Christmas, God!

HAPPY BIRTHDAY, !

Jesus

I'm so happy that Christmas is . . . FOR ME!

Christmas is . . . **For Me!**

What is your favorite Christmas symbol?